Seaside SANCTUARY

5650330342 815

Seaside Sanctuary is published by Stone Arch Books
A Capstone Imprint
1710 Roe Crest Drive
North Mankato, Minnesota 56003
www.mycapstone.com

Library of Congress Cataloging-in-Publication Data
Names: Berne, Emma Carlson, author. | Madrid, Erwin, illustrator.
Title: A dolphin named Star / by Emma Carlson Berne ; illustrated by
  Erwin Madrid.

Description: North Mankato, Minnesota : Stone Arch Books, [2019] |
  Series: Seaside sanctuary | Summary: Seaside Sanctuary Marine Wildlife
  Refuge in South Carolina has a wild pen that is supposed to be healthier for
  the marine animals brought there, but the three new dolphins are getting sick
  and no one can explain why; Elsa Roth, whose parents work at the sanctuary,
  is convinced that a local chemical plant is to blame, but since the water tests do
  not show contamination she is having trouble getting the adults to believe her—
  and if she is going to save a dolphin called Star she will have to find some way
  to prove her theory.

Identifiers: LCCN 2018037068 | ISBN 9781496578594 (hardcover) | ISBN
  9781496580283 (pbk.) | ISBN 9781496578631 (ebook pdf)
Subjects: LCSH: Dolphins—Juvenile fiction. | Marine parks and reserves—
  Juvenile fiction. | Wildlife rescue—Juvenile fiction. | Marine pollution—
  Juvenile fiction. | Waste disposal in the ocean—Juvenile fiction. | CYAC:
  Dolphins—Fiction. | Marine parks and reserves—Fiction. | Wildlife rescue—
  Fiction. | Marine pollution—Fiction. | Pollution—Fiction.
Classification: LCC PZ7.B455139 Do 2019 | DDC [Fic]—dc23
LC record available at https://lccn.loc.gov/2018037068

Designer: Aruna Rangarajan
Photo Credits: Shutterstock: Christina Li, (dolphin) 109, Color Brush, design element throughout, KRAUCHANKA HENADZ, design element throughout, Nikiparonak, design element throughout, Theeradech Sanin, design element throughout

Special thanks to Wayne McFee, research wildlife biologist at the National Oceanic and Atmospheric Administration's National Ocean Service, for his patience and expertise in answering many questions about dolphins and pollutants.

Printed in the United States of America.
1466

A Dolphin
Named Star

by Emma Carlson Berne
illustrated by Erwin Madrid

STONE ARCH BOOKS
a capstone imprint

Dear Diary,

    The past few months have been crazy, and not just because I moved across the country. I never thought we'd leave Chicago. The city was home my whole life. I loved the rumbling above-ground trains, the massive skyscrapers, the sidewalks filled with people. . . . Believe it or not, I even liked my school. It was the type of place where it was cool to be smart.

    But then, right after school ended for the year, Mom and Dad announced we were moving. They decided to leave their jobs as marine biologists at the Shedd Aquarium and move the whole family to Charleston, South Carolina! They both got jobs running someplace called Seaside Sanctuary Marine Wildlife Refuge—jobs that were "too good to pass up," as they put it.

    And at first, I couldn't believe Seaside Sanctuary would ever seem like home. Everything was different— the humidity, the salty air, the palmetto trees, the old brick streets lined with massive live oaks. Not to mention the flat, quiet beaches with water warm enough to swim in all year—you don't see that along Lake Michigan.

But it hasn't all been bad. For starters, I met my best friend, Olivia, on my first day at Seaside Sanctuary. She was sitting by the turtle pool, reading. By the end of the morning, I knew three very important things about Olivia:

1. Her older sister, Abby, is the vet at the sanctuary.
2. She doesn't like talking to people she doesn't know.
3. She wants to be a dolphin researcher when she grows up.

And I knew we were going to be best friends.

I still miss Chicago. But between helping the volunteers with feedings, cleaning tanks, showing tourists around, and prepping seal food in the industrial-sized blender, I haven't had much time to think about my old life. And one thing is for sure—at Seaside Sanctuary, I'm never lonely, and I'm never bored.

Chapter 1

"Olivia! They're here. The dolphins are here!"
I called from where I stood outside my best
friend's apartment.

Olivia swung open the front door before I even
finished talking and came racing out. "I'm coming!"

There was no time to waste. Today was a big
day. Seaside Sanctuary, the marine facility where
I lived with my parents, took in marine life that
had been injured in the wild or stranded on the

beaches. We had turtles, seals, otters—and today, three dolphins.

Olivia and I ran down the narrow apartment stairs, past the pools on the top floor, and down another staircase. We hurried past the closed tanks on the bottom floor, through the cement courtyard with the big pools and metal enclosures, and out to the sandy beach. We skidded to a halt at the edge of a rocky cove.

There, marine technicians from the dolphins' old facility were moving the dolphins from the back of a transport van that had been pulled up close to the edge. The animals lay in narrow canvas slings, floating in tanks just large enough for their bodies.

"Careful, please!" my mom called. She stood by the van door with Abby, Olivia's older sister and the sanctuary veterinarian.

Olivia and I crowded up beside them. I knew that if the dolphins moved around too much, they could hurt themselves. I held my breath as one by one, the animals were lowered into the netted cove that would be their new home.

"Why aren't they living in the tanks anymore?" Olivia asked her sister.

Abby looked up from her clipboard. "The sea pen will be healthier for them. They can move around, fish can swim in and out, and we can still feed and care for them. These three can't live in the wild again—they've been raised in captivity. But they'll have as good a life here as we can give them."

Olivia and I dropped to our stomachs, leaning over the water as techs released the canvas slings. The dolphins swam free, going from one end of the cove to the other, carefully exploring the rock walls and the netting at the front with their delicate, sensitive snouts.

"Hey, guys!" I called down to them. "Welcome to your new home!"

One of the dolphins blew a plume of water through her blowhole. I looked back at my mom with delight. "She answered me!"

"And that was polite of her, because *she* is actually a *he*." Mom looked down at her clipboard. "Meet Star. He's about ten years old. We've tagged each of their dorsal fins—Star has a blue tag."

"And the other ones? Are they girls or boys?" Olivia asked. "They're sooo cute."

Abby clicked her tongue. "Male or female, Olivia! I know I've said this before, but I'll say it again. These dolphins may have been raised in captivity, but they are wild animals. They are not pets or toys. They're very strong, and they could hurt you, so respect them. It's important not to anthropomorphize animals, you know. They're not people, and we shouldn't treat them as if they were. Anyway, the yellow and red tags are both females: Sunshine and Ruby."

Anthropomorphize. I filed that word away in the back of my mind to look up online when I got home.

Olivia nodded at her sister and looked away. I nudged her shoulder. Olivia looked over, and I rolled my eyes, tipping my head toward Abby. Olivia's big sister was super smart and knew everything about marine animals, but she could be a little *overly* serious sometimes.

Olivia smiled at me, and we flopped on our stomachs again to admire the dolphins. They were now diving to the bottom of the cove to test out the depth.

The tech slammed the van doors. "Driveway clear now? We could hardly get around that other van earlier. It was blocking our way."

Mom looked puzzled. "What van?" she asked.

The tech climbed into the driver's seat while the others piled into the back. He started the engine and stuck his head out the window. "Your white van. It was pulled off to the side, but it was still in the way."

Mom shook her head. "We don't have a white van."

But the truck was already roaring away. Before Mom could say anything else, we spotted Dad coming down from the office. A woman I didn't recognize was beside him.

"Mae, this is Delilah Germaine," Dad said, pushing his glasses up his nose. "She's on the board of the local Wildlife Resources chapter. You might remember her. She was here when we came in for the interview."

"Oh, yes!" Mom reached out to shake Ms. Germaine's hand.

"Wildlife Resources just gave a large donation to Seaside Sanctuary," Dad said. "I'm told Ms. Germaine spoke up on our behalf."

I sat up. Ms. Germaine was younger than my parents, with dark lipstick and dangly earrings. She wore a silk wrap dress and was looking around at everything.

"We always visit the groups we donate to," Ms. Germaine said. "It was my lucky day when I was asked to do the visit to your sanctuary. You have a very impressive set-up. Everything is in lovely shape."

"Have you seen the turtle tanks?" Mom asked. "We just had them installed last week. And this is our very newest addition—a sheltered wild pen. We just took on three captive dolphins this morning."

Ms. Germaine must not have noticed the dolphins before because she stepped forward and peered over the edge of the cove, then jumped back as if startled. "Oh!" she exclaimed. "The dolphins are in there!"

"Well, yes." Mom looked confused. "This wild pen is unique. It's one of only a few in the country. We had to get a federal permit to build it. It'll be a much healthier environment for our dolphins."

"Oh! Of course." Ms. Germaine seemed worried, but I couldn't figure out why. "I just assumed they'd be in a tank at the facility. That's your standard practice, isn't it?"

"Yes, usually," Abby chimed in. "But Mae is right. This is a wonderful environment for our dolphins. We're so lucky to have gotten the permit for the wild pen."

"That is lucky." Ms. Germaine fiddled with her earring. "I'm sure Wildlife Resources will be delighted too. Well! Thank you for the lovely tour. I'm afraid I must be off!"

Olivia and I watched as Dad walked Ms. Germaine to her car at the front gate. "She's kind of weird," Olivia said.

I nodded. "Maybe she's just nervous. Or maybe she's not used to animals, like we are." I leaned over the edge of the cove again. "That's too bad."

Chapter 2

"OK, you two, here's your first assignment."
Abby handed me a green cooler. Inside, I knew,
would be ice and a tray with fat herring—dead,
but still fresh.

The summer sun was bright and hot on my
head, and it was only eight o'clock in the morning.
Olivia and I were starting our first day with the
dolphins, and Mom had asked us to help Abby.
Since it was summer break, our days were wide

open. We wanted to be the first ones down to the cove.

"Breakfast time, guys!" Olivia tried to heft the cooler and almost dropped it. "Whoops."

"Careful." Abby led us to the edge of the cove, and we all looked down into the green-gray water. The dolphins were swimming at the surface, their red, yellow, and blue dorsal tags clearly visible.

"We need to get these guys used to us," Abby explained. "They've been around humans all their lives, but when dolphins come to a new place, you almost have to start the process all over again. Later we'll go out on the boat near the cove, but right now they need to get used to us and to the feeding system."

Half an hour later, Olivia and I were sitting quietly cross-legged at the edge of the cove. The cooler sat between us, just as Abby had instructed.

Every now and then, we would take out a fish and wave it gently, just below the surface of the water. So far the dolphins had ignored the fish, which were starting to get a little tattered.

I kept my eyes fixed on the animals. The dolphins kept swimming up and lifting their heads out of the water to see us.

"Oh, Liv, look at Star." The blue-tagged dolphin swam toward us and then away, as if trying to get our attention. He made a soft clicking sound as he swam—his echolocation, I knew.

"He's so beautiful," Olivia said. "Look how bright his eyes are—like stars."

I wiggled on my stomach until my face was near the cove water. "Star. Star, we're your friends. Please, have a fish."

Star swam a little closer. He made another clicking noise.

"Star." I made my voice very low and very quiet. Dolphins had super listening. They were sensitive to any changes in people's voices. "Here's a fish."

Olivia sat very still. Her eyes were fixed on the water. "He's listening."

Slowly I held out the fish. Star lifted his head and opened his mouth. Barely breathing, I laid the fish inside. He closed his jaws and splashed back down into the water.

"He did it!" I whispered. I wanted to yell, but that would frighten the dolphins and undo all our hard work. I settled for squeezing Olivia's arm.

"Let's try some more," Olivia said. "Now that Star is eating, maybe the others will follow." She scooted closer to the edge with the bucket.

Star and Ruby both swam up this time. Olivia held out a fish to each. The dolphins snapped them up.

I admired the power of those sleek gray bodies. Dolphins always looked like they were smiling because of the way their mouths were. But I knew that while they were social, curious animals, they could also be powerful killing machines and deadly hunters.

"Liv, look." I pointed. Sunshine was floating near the cove net, ignoring the other two dolphins. "Why isn't she coming over?"

"I don't know." Olivia stared at the dolphin. "She doesn't seem interested. Maybe we should get my sister."

Olivia hurried off and returned just as quickly. Abby was behind her, struggling into a wet suit. "I'm going to go in and see if I can get a closer look at her." She quickly fixed a mask and a snorkel and slid into the water.

Olivia and I leaned over the cove edge. Abby swam over to the pen, staying outside the netting, and swam back and forth, looking carefully but not touching the dolphin. Sunshine barely moved.

After a few minutes, Abby swam back to us and hauled herself out of the water. "She's lethargic," she said back onshore, pushing her mask up. "Eyes half-closed, and she's staying at the surface."

"What does that mean?" I asked.

"That she doesn't have energy to dive. She's trying to make breathing easy on herself. And to be honest, I'm concerned about the other two as well." Abby pulled her mask free of her wet, tangled hair and pushed her wet suit off. "Their energy seems low. And the blue-tag has sores on his underside—I saw them when I dove down."

"Here, I'll hang that up." Olivia took the wet suit from her sister.

"Thanks. I need to look a few things up." Abby strode quickly toward the office. All of her focus was clearly on figuring out what was wrong with the dolphins.

I sniffed. "Are you wearing perfume?"

"No." Olivia looked horrified. "Why would I wear perfume?"

"Something smells funny." I leaned over and sniffed at my friend. "It's the wet suit." I put my nose down to the wet neoprene and inhaled. "Yuck! It smells all chemical-y. Like a factory."

I'd been around enough wet suits to know that they normally smelled like seaweed and ocean water, not chemicals. There was something else there too, something from my past. I couldn't quite figure out what it was, but in some weird way it reminded me of Mom.

Olivia sniffed too. "You're right. That's weird. It was hanging up with the others."

"Maybe it got mildewed." We started up to the office. "We can let it dry outside."

But as we walked, my mind kept returning to the smell. What did it remind me of? The thought tugged at the edge of my mind all the way back to the office.

Chapter 3

Olivia burst through the door the next morning as I was eating my oatmeal. "The dolphins have gotten worse." She slumped down in the chair. "Your mom's already down at the cove with my sister."

"I thought she was in the bathroom!" I pushed back my chair and bolted from the kitchen, Olivia close behind.

At the cove edge, I skidded to a stop. I didn't need to be a vet to see that the dolphins were very sick. All three of them floated limply, seeming barely to keep themselves at the surface of the water. Worst of all, I could see pink sores dotting their bodies. Suddenly something cloudy appeared in the water near Star's head.

"Vomiting." Abby shook her head. She looked as if she'd barely combed her hair that morning. "They're sick, but with what?"

"They need tests, but I don't want to pull them from the water," Mom said. Her face was creased with worry. "The stress of an exam could hurt them even worse. They'll need close monitoring. I don't think I should go to this dinner tonight. Warren can go and take the girls. They'll represent us."

"What dinner?" I asked.

Mom turned as if she'd just remembered I was standing there. "It's a beneficiary dinner for all the groups Wildlife Resources supports. They're one of our biggest donors. At least, they are now. They never gave much before, but a few months ago, we got a huge gift from them. One of the biggest they gave this year. Anyway, you and Olivia go with Dad, OK? Abby and I will stay with the dolphins."

⌒

That evening, I found myself perched at the edge of a gilt chair in a fancy ballroom at the Charleston Inn. Beside me, Olivia tugged at the waist of her dress. "This dress is making me itchy," she whispered.

"Mine too," I whispered back. I hadn't worn my pink dress since my cousin's wedding last year. I must have grown since then because the dress was tight under the arms.

All around us, well-dressed grown-ups filled the round tables. At the podium, various speakers went on and on about money and gifts—not the interesting kind—until I thought I was going to pass out right there at the table and fall to the floor. I tried to stay awake by making a little house with the butter pats, but then Dad gave me a stern look. My construction project was over.

A man in a gray suit stepped up to the microphone. "And now I'd like to introduce Delilah Germaine. Ms. Germaine is the plant manager for Charleston Area Chemical Manufacturing, Inc., located right here in town, at the edge of the James Island Waterway. She is also on the Wildlife Resources board. We would like to thank Ms. Germaine and her boss, plant owner William Stanton, for being here tonight. Ms. Germaine." He stepped aside.

I craned my neck. Ms. Germaine was making her way to the front, wearing a dark silk dress that made her look like a Greek goddess.

She didn't mention working for a chemical company when she stopped by the sanctuary, I thought.

A grumpy-looking man with a brooding face and hair combed straight back sat at the table she'd just left.

That must be Mr. Stanton, I thought.

"Thank you." At the podium, Ms. Germaine cleared her throat and unfolded her notes with a little rustle. "We are so glad to be here tonight."

I leaned back in my chair as Ms. Germaine spoke and wondered how the dolphins were doing. Those sores had looked so uncomfortable. I'd had a sore on my hand once, and it had hurt like crazy.

Suddenly, I sat straight up in my chair. Sores! Hands! Gloves! In an instant, I realized what I'd smelled on the wet suit.

"Olivia!" I whispered frantically. "Bathroom, now!"

Olivia knew not to ask any questions. Quickly and quietly, we stood up from our table, making our way through the crowded ballroom and out the big double doors.

"What is it?" Olivia asked as soon as we were out in the hall. She glanced around to make sure no one was nearby.

"I know what that smell on the wet suit was— *gasoline*!" I exclaimed. "It didn't hit me until just now. My mom used to have these black gloves she'd wear whenever she was pumping gas because she didn't like the smell to get on her hands. When I smelled the wet suit, it reminded me of her for some reason, but I couldn't figure out why at first. But that has to be it!"

Olivia's brow furrowed. "But why would the wet suit smell—wait!" She snapped her fingers. "It wasn't the wet suit—it was the *water* that smelled like gas."

"The water that the dolphins were swimming in—*are* swimming in." I felt like a real-life detective.

At that moment, a burst of applause came from behind the closed doors, followed by a chatter of voices. The big doors opened and people started to filter out.

"It's over," Olivia said. "Now we can get back and talk to my sister."

"Did you enjoy the presentation, girls?" Ms. Germaine asked, walking up behind Olivia. The grumpy Mr. Stanton was beside her.

"Oh yes," I lied. "Very interesting."

"Come along, Ms. Germaine," Stanton said through his teeth.

But Ms. Germaine lingered. "How . . . how are the dolphins?" she asked.

I shook my head. "Not good. They're really sick. They have sores on their bodies, and they're vomiting. We're trying to find out what's wrong with them."

"Oh!" Ms. Germaine took a sudden step back. "Oh, I'm so sorry to hear that." She did look sorry—and worried. She wiped her hands on her silky dress. Streaks of moisture showed up on the light fabric.

"I'm sorry, we really must be going," Mr. Stanton growled. He marched off down the hall, pushing his way through the crowd of people.

Ms. Germaine looked after him. "I'm the driver, so I have to go as well. I . . ." She hesitated. "I'm sorry to hear about the dolphins."

Without another word, she rushed down the hall after her boss.

Olivia and I looked at each other. "She's really upset," Olivia said.

"Yeah," I agreed. "Well, I can understand that. Think of how upset we've been. And she saw the dolphins in person too. She probably loves animals just as much as we do."

Olivia considered that. "Probably."

"Come on, I see my dad," I said. "I can't wait to get out of this itchy dress."

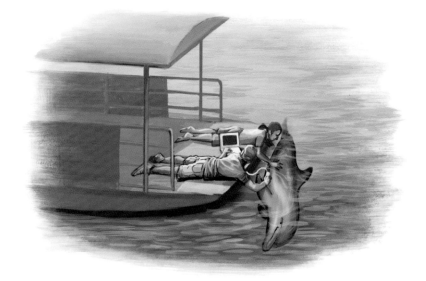

Chapter 4

Abby sat hunched over a stack of papers,
talking on the phone, when Olivia and I found
her in the office the next morning. The small
space was jammed with journals on marine
biology, piles of forms, and a dusty old computer
that shut off on its own. One wall was lined with
photos of every animal Seaside Sanctuary had
ever taken in.

"Mae, I didn't take a delivery this morning. Not that early," Abby said, talking to my mom, I realized. "Well, it wasn't the delivery van. His is blue, not white." She paused. "No. No. Maybe some sightseers. You know they come out this time of year. OK. I'll tell them not to park there if I see it again." She put the phone down. "What is it, girls?"

Abby listened patiently as we told her what we'd realized the night before—that there must be gas in the water. But I had barely finished before Abby shook her head.

"I'm sorry. Elsa's mom and I already thought of that. We took a water sample yesterday. The usual array of pollutants are in the pen, unfortunately, but nothing at levels that could cause this kind of illness."

"Then what was that smell on the wet suit?" I asked. I wasn't ready to give up on our theory.

"I don't know—maybe the neoprene itself? They are new. It might have been off-gassing. Objects made of plastic or other man-made materials sometimes release gases like that shortly after they're made." She sighed and checked an appointment book on the desk. "Dr. Lampe, the dolphin specialist, is coming soon. He's going to perform an in-water ultrasound. Maybe that will give us some answers."

As we left the room, I caught Abby's last words: "Because they don't have much time left."

Fear gripped me. "Liv!" I exclaimed. "We've got to investigate!"

Olivia nodded, and together we raced back up the stairs to the apartment. We shut the door to my room and opened my laptop.

"OK. Let's see what we can find for *gas smell in water*." I scanned the search results. "Nothing. It's like stuff for water in your house."

Olivia leaned over my shoulder. "Try *gas smell in ocean*."

I typed it in. "Oil spill. Gas leaks. No, no. It's a lot of stuff about oil spills—wait!" I clicked on a link. "Look at this. PAH. Polycyclic aromatic hydrocarbons."

"What does that even mean?" Olivia asked, furrowing her brow.

"Ugh, there's a lot of info." I scanned the page. "OK, so it sounds like PAHs are leftovers from when you make chemicals or burn coal or tar." I kept reading. "They can be in a gas form or a liquid form. And they sound nasty. They can cause cancer and all kinds of other health problems in humans *and animals*." I inhaled. "And listen to this! If PAHs show up in the ocean, marine mammals might act confused and lethargic. They could also throw up and get *skin lesions*." I looked up. "That's skin sores!"

"Those are almost exactly the symptoms the dolphins have been showing!" Olivia exclaimed.

"And get this," I continued. "PAHs evaporate fast. Because of that, you can often smell them on the surface of the water. This must be what's in the water!"

Olivia made a face. "But wait. Remember what my sister said? They did a test for pollutants already."

"Oh yeah." I sank back on the bed. "Ugh, I need a break. My brain hurts."

"You want to go check on the dolphins? See how they're doing?" Olivia suggested. "Maybe that will help clear our minds."

I sat up. "Good idea."

We wandered back to the dolphin pen, not saying much. Dr. Lampe was there, just climbing into one of the boats with Abby.

"Dr. Lampe is going to examine their lungs using the portable ultrasound machine," Abby called.

I crouched down at the edge of the rocks with Olivia beside me. Sunshine and Ruby were floating at the surface of the water, barely moving. Their skin was still crusted with sores. Star swam slowly nearby. We watched him bump into the rock wall as if he couldn't even see it.

"Oh, Star!" I whispered. "I wish I could help you!"

Olivia patted my back. "Oh no. Look." She pointed.

Star was trying to blow out of his blowhole, but his exhalation was raspy and wet sounding. Then he chuffed, sending out a burst of air in an attempt to clear out his clogged breathing. Mucus lay in a spray around his blowhole opening.

I gasped. "He sounds terrible!"

We watched Abby steer the boat near Sunshine. Dr. Lampe reached over and placed the ultrasound wand on the dolphin's back. He slid it slowly on the skin while he and Abby watched the dark screen. Sunshine seemed too weak to swim away.

Finally Abby guided the boat back toward the dock. She and Dr. Lampe climbed out.

"Her lungs are definitely affected," the doctor told Abby. Olivia and I sat up and inched closer, listening. "It's no wonder she's having trouble breathing. You already checked for water pollutants?"

Abby nodded and spread her hands helplessly. "We took all the usual samples. Nothing out of the ordinary. If there was a leak into the cove, we would have picked that up."

Dr. Lampe nodded. "I agree. We'll have to keep treating the symptoms until we can find a diagnosis." He gave Abby a few more instructions, then climbed into his car and drove away.

"Abby!" Mom appeared at the top of the slope. "Can you come help me tube-feed the river otters? They're slippery little guys."

Abby gave us a sympathetic look, squeezed Olivia's shoulder, then trotted toward Mom. I lay on my stomach, watching the dolphins, head on my folded hands. I took a deep breath of the briny air and watched Star's cool gray back in the water below. Sunlight sparkled on the ocean surface like a handful of glitter.

Just a few hundred feet away, the mouth of the James Island Waterway spilled into the sea, browner than the ocean water, spreading out in a plume. I stared at the river opening. Something. Something about the waterway. James Island—

"Olivia!" I bolted upright. "It *has* to be a pollutant! Remember at the dinner? The guy said Charleston Area Chemical Manufacturing was on the *James Island Waterway*—right here!" I pointed.

"If a chemical was leaking from the factory, it would trickle down the waterway and spill out— right into the cove!"

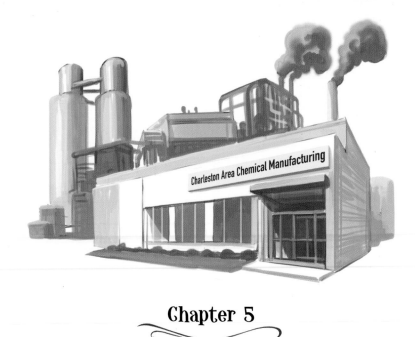

Chapter 5

I leaned forward as Mom steered our car smoothly into a parking space in front of a hulking plant. The silver letters over the big glass front doors spelled out *Charleston Area Chemical Manufacturing*.

"Come on, girls, Ms. Germaine is expecting us," Mom said, turning off the car and climbing out of the driver's seat.

"Do you really think we'll find some clue to the pollutants here?" Olivia whispered as we piled out of the back seat.

"Yes!" I insisted quietly. "There has to be a leak somewhere. I know it!" We walked into the lobby, which was big and cool and looked like an office building.

"Dr. Roth, girls!" Ms. Germaine called from across the room. She clicked across the tile on high heels. "What a pleasure to see you. I was thrilled to hear you wanted a tour."

"The girls were excited to see the plant." Mom smiled. "I was a little surprised. Elsa's never shown much interest in engineering before."

"It was me, really, Dr. Roth," Olivia quickly volunteered. "I've been reading this book all about factories, so I thought it would be fun to see a real one inside."

I glanced at my friend. "Nice," I whispered as we followed the grown-ups through a second set of glass doors at the other end of the lobby. "Good cover."

"Anything for the dolphins," Olivia whispered back. She didn't usually talk much in front of strangers, especially grown-ups.

Ms. Germaine led the way into a small room, where she outfitted us in white suits like hazmat workers, shoe covers, hair nets, and clear goggles. "Just a precaution," she explained. "The chemicals are all contained, of course."

I gave Olivia a look.

The factory floor was vast, soaring six stories high. White metal walkways lined the walls and crisscrossed overhead. Huge steel tanks, all with rows of dials on the outside, stood in rows with pipes extending from their sides. Workers in white suits adjusted the dials, consulted clipboards, or drove forklifts loaded with blue plastic barrels across the concrete floor.

"This is where the magic happens." Ms. Germaine gestured around her. "CACM makes twelve different kinds of chemicals. Most are used in plastics manufacturing and energy plants."

Mom smiled. "It certainly is an impressive setup." She and Ms. Germaine began to stroll slowly around the factory floor. Olivia and I trailed behind.

"Look for clues," I muttered out of the corner of my mouth.

"Like what?" Olivia whispered back. "A sign saying, *We Are Polluters?*"

"I don't know! Just anything." I scanned the floor and the walls as we walked. Olivia was right. What clues did I expect to find? Maybe this was a stupid idea after all.

My heart sank. I had dragged everyone out here on a wild goose chase while the dolphins were suffering back at home. What a waste of time.

"It's so helpful to have a strong community partner like CACM," Mom was saying to Ms. Germaine when I tuned back in. "So many factories have no interest in conservation. But with its strong support of Wildlife Resources and Seaside Sanctuary, CACM has really made it a priority."

Ms. Germaine smiled. She didn't seem to know what to say. I noticed that she had dark circles of sweat under the arms of her dress. Maybe she needed a stronger deodorant.

"This is the main floor, as you can see," Ms. Germaine told us. "The chemicals run through the pipes here and into storage barrels." She pointed to a hundred or so blue barrels lined up with pipes feeding into the tops. "The chemicals are then transported to the buyer." She pushed open a heavy steel door. "This is where the barrels are loaded."

Olivia and I peered through the door. There wasn't much to see. A few pallets of the blue barrels, a line of white vans. Some had their doors open, probably waiting for loading. A line of drips led from one of the pallets to the back of a van where a worker was loading a barrel.

I tried to think. If there was a pollutant leak, it would be in one of the pipes. And if there was a leak, did anyone know about it? Maybe a pipe had fractured, and no one at the factory knew. There was only one way to find out.

"So . . . where is the waterway from here?" I tried to sound cool, but Mom and Ms. Germaine both turned and stared at me as if surprised.

"Very smooth," Olivia whispered.

I tried to recover. "I just love to see the water!" I knew I sounded bizarre, but I didn't care. Grown-ups never thought kids had any serious thoughts anyway.

"It's over here." Ms. Germaine led us back across the main factory floor.

As we passed a glassed-in office area, I spotted Mr. Stanton, the factory owner, looking out at us. He must have been watching because he offered a brief, unsmiling nod as we passed.

"That creepy man is staring at us," Olivia whispered.

"I know. He's such a weirdo. He never smiles," I whispered back as Ms. Germaine led us out another door on the opposite side of the factory floor.

"Here we are," Ms. Germaine said.

We were standing on a walkway that ran along one of the factory walls. In front of us, down a steep embankment, the James Island Waterway glinted in the bright South Carolina sun. A few miles away, I knew, its waters spilled into the dolphin cove. Poking out from the side of the building were elbows of the white pipes we'd seen inside. They bent back into the building, as if the factory wasn't big enough to contain them.

"Very pleasant." Mom looked around approvingly.

Quickly I tried to look for any sign of leaks in the pipes. Out of the corner of my eye, I could see Olivia doing the same. But everything looked dry and tight. There was no moisture visible anywhere.

I couldn't take it anymore. "Do you ever have leaking pipes?" I blurted out in desperation.

Ms. Germaine looked down at me. Something passed over her face that I couldn't read.

"Elsa!" Mom said. She looked horrified. "What are you saying?"

"Nothing. I just wondered." My face was flaming. Out of the corner of my eye, I could see Olivia looking away over the water.

"It's all right," Ms. Germaine said. "Elsa's asking good questions. And the answer is we do, occasionally. But we take leaks very seriously. That's why we had this meter installed by the local EPA." She pointed to a device sticking up from the waterway. "It measures all pollutants in the water. If there was a leak, the meter would show increased levels. As you can see, the numbers read zero." She exhaled as if having given a long speech.

"I'm sure they do," Mom agreed, giving me a dirty look. "Please excuse my daughter. CACM has been a friend and partner of Seaside Sanctuary for quite some time now. We have you to thank for many of the improvements in our facility. I am sure my daughter will be glad to be reminded of that."

I cringed. This hadn't gone at all as I'd hoped. We hadn't found a thing, and I'd upset my mom. Back in the car, after saying our goodbyes to Ms. Germaine, Olivia and I sat silently as Mom lectured us from the front seat.

"And are you trying to suggest that the factory is doing something illegal with their chemicals? Because if I thought that was the reason for this trip, I certainly would not have taken you. Or you, Olivia."

"But, Mom, we were just thinking—"

Mom shot us a look in the rear-view mirror. "I'm sure I don't need to remind you two that Seaside Sanctuary is a non-profit. We need donors to stay open. CACM's money bought the new industrial blender and coolers. It also paid for the herring and other fish the mammals eat. High-quality frozen fish is one of our biggest costs. And you know the blenders for the liquid food are very expensive. Not to mention the coolers and trays, which are important for feeding the dolphins, otters, and pelicans. We have CACM to thank for the food our animals are eating."

"I know," I mumbled.

Olivia and I stared out our windows. I'd been so sure we were going to find the answers we needed at the factory. Now we were back to the beginning—and the dolphins were only getting worse.

Chapter 6

"But if it's a disease, why can't they find out what it is?" I asked for what felt like the tenth time. As I spoke, I lifted out another tray of herring from the huge Styrofoam cooler and laid it on the counter.

"I don't know. Maybe they haven't looked hard enough?" Olivia held up the first fish in the row and examined it carefully.

We were in the sanctuary kitchen, where the dolphin's food was prepped. They ate herring because it was full of fat, which dolphins needed to keep them floating in the water. This wasn't just any herring, though—it was special herring all the way from the North Atlantic. It was caught and frozen right on the boat so all the good nutrients were preserved.

The fish was trucked in from Rhode Island on ice, and every single fish was inspected by hand. If any had holes or eyes missing, it was tossed. Bacteria and microbes from the ocean could have gotten into those holes. Since the dolphins were from a different part of the ocean, they could get sick if they ingested any of those things.

"I think your sister could find a disease if there was one," I argued. I held up a herring. "Missing eye on this one." I tossed it into a discard bucket nearby.

"Then what?" Olivia started lifting the inspected fish into the dolphins' individual coolers. Each one was labeled with a name. Inside was a layer of ice, then a tray. A label on the outside said how many fish each dolphin got.

"I don't know," I admitted. I hated to give up the idea of a pollutant, but after the visit to the factory I had to admit that it looked like a dead end. Dry pipes and the water meter *and* water samples were hard to ignore.

"Girls, are you done here?" Abby came through the door. I'd never seen the vet look so haggard. Her normally cheerful, tanned face was lined, and her hair was unwashed. She looked as if she hadn't slept in days.

"How are they?" I almost didn't want to hear the answer.

Abby shook her head. "Not good. Sunshine is worse. The others are holding steady, at least, but that's not saying much. They were already very sick." She hesitated. "Girls, come here." She pulled out a plastic chair and sat down, her head bent and her hands dangling between her knees.

Olivia and I exchanged a look and pulled up chairs. Foreboding churned in my stomach.

"I'm not going to hide this from you girls," Abby said. "The dolphins are extremely sick. They might die. All of them."

"No!" The word burst from me. I stood up, knocking over my chair. "They can't! Abby! You'll save them!"

Abby shook her head slowly. "I'm trying. I am. But even with all my training and knowledge there's something here I just can't figure out. I don't know what's making them sick. And meanwhile, they're not getting any better."

I looked at Olivia, who was still seated, slumped down in her chair. Tears were trickling

down her cheeks in long streams. She didn't
bother to wipe them away.

༄

I sat cross-legged on my bed the next morning.
The clock beside me read 6 a.m., but I'd already
been up for an hour, thinking and doodling in the
notebook on my knees. I'd had a terrible night,
with visions of pipes and deadly streams of liquid
and sick dolphins occupying my dreams.

Now I looked down at the paper where I'd
drawn a box labeled *CACM*—Charleston Area
Chemical Manufacturing. A dotted line and an
arrow pointed to another box labeled *SS* for
Seaside Sanctuary.

Slowly I drew a big X through the line. There
was no leak, and no connection.

I sighed and laid down the pen. I was at a dead
end.

Suddenly the door flew open. Olivia stood there, her face pale, her hair mussed as if she'd just woken up.

"Oh, Elsa!" she sobbed. She started to say something else but couldn't get the words out. She didn't have to. I just knew.

Together we raced down to the cove.

Dad stood to one side, bent over something I couldn't see. Abby and Dr. Lampe were already in the boat. Beside me, Olivia groped for my hand.

Sunshine floated in the water, belly-up, her dorsal fin under the water.

My breath rasped in my throat. I couldn't stand the sight. I turned away, my eyes dry and scratchy, like sandpaper.

"I know." Mom put her hand softly on my back. "It's terrible to see. I hate to think of her suffering." Her voice broke.

Together we watched as Abby and Dr. Lampe knelt on the mat, which supported their weight as well as Sunshine's. Dr. Lampe started examining the dead animal, talking in a low voice to Abby, who took notes on a small, waterproof laptop.

Star and Ruby floated in the water nearby. They didn't seem to have the strength to swim or do much of anything else. But they were alive. That was something, at least.

Dad lifted what had been in his hands, and I realized it was the big camera, the SLR they usually kept in the office. He aimed it toward Sunshine and took several shots before I flew at him.

"What are you doing!" I screamed. "Stop taking pictures of her! She's dead! Dad, she's dead!" I grabbed his arm so hard that he almost dropped the camera.

Dad turned, and I fell back, surprised by the anger in his face. "I know she's dead! And we have to document it, Elsa. We're scientists. It's our job. Now get off my arm. You're not the only one who's sad here." He turned back to the water without another word and lifted the camera to his eye again.

Something broke inside me, and I collapsed onto the ground, head in hands, and sobbed. For a long time, the only sound was my weeping. Then I sensed someone close beside me. I opened my eyes. It was Olivia. Her face looked just as anguished as I felt. But more than that she looked mad.

"Elsa, we *have* to save the others. We *have* to find out what's making them sick. I won't do anything else until we do," she whispered fiercely. "Whether you help me or not."

I lifted my head. "I'll help. Of course I'll help."

"Star and Ruby need us. Don't give up!" Olivia said.

"I won't." As I spoke, I felt determination flowing back into me. I wouldn't give up—not on Olivia and definitely not on the dolphins.

Chapter 7

"Come on. Please, Star." I leaned over the edge of the motorboat where it floated just inside the cove netting and held a fat, glistening herring out over the water.

It was seven in the morning, and Olivia and I had been first down to the cove again. Abby said we could be the ones to try to give the dolphins their breakfast.

"Come on, eat, Star!" Olivia said beside me. She reached into the open cooler that held Star and Ruby's breakfast and pulled out another herring.

At the bow of the boat, Abby sighed. "Let's get a little closer, girls. They're just too weak to swim that far." She maneuvered the boat a little closer to the sick dolphins.

Sunshine's body was gone. Dr. Lampe had taken her with him when he left a few hours ago. And Abby had let us go out into the boat for feeding in an attempt at keeping our spirits up. But it wasn't much of a spirit-booster when the remaining two dolphins were so sick they could hardly swim.

I swished the fish gently back and forth in the water, the signal for feeding, and at last, Star swam over. As if it cost him great effort, he lifted his head out of the water and opened his mouth, the signal he was ready for the fish.

I cringed at the sight of the sores on his body—they were almost like wounds now. There was a thick layer of mucus splattered around his blowhole, and I could hear him struggling to breathe.

As I placed the fish in his mouth, I noticed Olivia leaning way over the edge of the boat. She was subtly sniffing at the surface of the water.

"Smell anything?" I whispered as she sat up.

Olivia wrinkled her forehead. "I'm not really sure . . . there is a kind of gassy smell when you get your nose right down there, but it's not as strong as the other day. I don't know—maybe it was always there and I just never noticed it before?"

Star's body bumped the boat, sending it rocking gently, and I reached down. I stroked the top of his nose, his rubbery skin squeaking beneath my fingers. I was reminded all over again of how powerful the dolphins were. Star's muscles flexed like steel springs under his skin. If he weren't so sick, he could shoot through the water to grab fish with incredible speed.

"Oh no." Abby was staring toward the shore.

I followed her gaze and saw Mom standing on the cove edge, waving at us. Even this far away I could see her face was strained.

"That doesn't look good." Abby started the motor and steered us back to the dock. "What is it, Mae?" she asked as we climbed out.

"Come into the office," Mom said.

Abby followed Mom, and they disappeared through the doorway. After a moment, Olivia and I followed too. We found them crouched over the computer.

"The news about Sunshine's death has made it to the press," Mom said when we came in. "The *Post and Courier* has a pretty bad opinion piece."

I frowned. The *Post and Courier* was Charleston's daily newspaper. If news of Sunshine's death had appeared there, the whole city would have heard about it by now.

Abby scanned the online article while we looked over her shoulder. "'What's Gone Wrong at Seaside Sanctuary?'" she read aloud. "'Showpiece Marine Mammal Dies Under Mysterious Circumstances.'"

"Mysterious circumstances!" I looked up at Mom. "She was sick!"

Mom shook her head, looking as upset as I felt. "I know, honey."

I kept reading over Abby's shoulder. "Seaside Sanctuary . . . leading Charleston area marine sanctuary . . . gravely ill dolphins . . . one of three wild pens on the Eastern coastline . . . marine biologists and sanctuary managers Drs. Mae and Warren Roth responsible for overseeing operations and making decisions about animals' health. This incident calls into question whether the sanctuary is qualified . . . authorities have been notified . . ."

I looked up, stricken. "They're talking about you and Dad! Saying you're not qualified?" I scanned the page again. "That doesn't make any sense! It wasn't your fault Sunshine died! They won't shut us down, will they?"

"Not based on this article alone," Mom replied. But I could see she was worried.

I felt myself trembling. Seaside Sanctuary was home. Someone couldn't really take it away, could they? "We're trying our best! We love the dolphins! How could anyone think we didn't care about them?"

Mom shook her head. "People feel strongly about animals like dolphins and elephants and lions. We call them 'charismatic mammals.' They're charming and appealing, which makes them a big draw for zoos and sanctuaries. They help us fund other, less charismatic creatures like insects and fish. But that's why people are so upset. They take the deaths of these animals seriously. Just like we do. And we will figure this out. Don't worry."

But before I could respond, Dad called down from the office. "Mae? Could you come up here right away?"

My eyes met Olivia's. Something was wrong. Very wrong. We jumped up and trotted after Mom and Abby as they walked quickly up the hill.

A man wearing a brown shirt and tie and holding a clipboard was standing in the office. I noticed immediately that he was wearing rubber boots, which looked odd with his dress shirt.

"Dr. Roth?" The man extended his hand. "Tom Clark. Inspector from the Department of Fisheries and Agriculture."

"Oh! Oh, hello." Mom sounded anxious.

I stepped on Olivia's foot and felt her nudge me in response. What was an inspector doing here? Was he going to shut us down?

"We understand that one of your three bottlenose dolphins has died. We're sorry to hear that. I'm here to run through the protocol, you understand. Just make sure everything is up to snuff at your facility." He spoke in a brisk, clipped way.

I saw him take a quick look around the stuffed office with its piles of papers and files and its ancient, yellowing desktop computer. He made a mark on his clipboard. Was that bad? Was something wrong with the office?

"Of course. We understand." Mom sounded calm, but I could see a little muscle jumping in her neck. "Please come with us. Dr. Roth and I will be happy to show you the facility."

Olivia and I started to follow as they filed out the door, but Mom turned around. "You girls stay back," she murmured. "This is official business, OK?"

I sank back into a chair. Bits of down still poked out from when an injured pelican had gotten in here last month. Olivia perched on another chair and drew her feet up under her chin.

"What do you think he's looking at?" I said, examining my toenails. "Like how clean the pens are? They're so clean! Oh, Liv, what if Star dies? Or Ruby? What if they shut us down? What would happen to all the other animals? They'd be homeless!"

I swallowed hard at the thought of the river otters wandering the streets of Charleston at night, lonely, scared, looking through trashcans for food. Of course, I knew that wouldn't really happen, but the image was hard to erase.

A few minutes later, the outer door to the office banged. Mom came in, followed by Abby and Dad. Elsa and Olivia sat up.

"How was it?" I asked tentatively. I held my breath.

Mom dropped into a chair. She rested her elbows on her knees and stared at the floor. "Pretty bad," she said finally. "We're going to be reviewed at the next board meeting."

"Oh no!" Olivia cried out. "What does that mean?"

Dad crossed the room and patted us both on our backs. "Nothing yet." I caught a glance he sent to Abby. "It'll mean more inspectors. They'll be looking through everything—our maintenance, our feeding systems, our staff, volunteers, you name it." He hesitated. "But even if everything is perfect, they could still shut us down."

I wanted to leap up from my seat, but Dad's face stopped me. He looked like an old man. The grief slowly drained out of me as I stared at him, replaced with a burning, quiet rage.

Olivia and I were going to save the other dolphins. We were going to find out what was making them sick. I was going to fix that look on my dad's face. I was going to save Seaside Sanctuary.

Chapter 8

Olivia rubbed her eyes. "Are we really staying here all night?" she asked, yawning and reaching for the can of Coke sitting on a stack of journals.

"All night—or until we find the answer," I replied.

I tossed a copy of *Proceedings of the Society of Marine Biologists* onto a massive pile in one corner of the office and grabbed another one from the stack. I flipped quickly to the table of contents and ran a finger down the list of chapter titles.

"Flipper deformities, red vs. white herring, communication dialect found . . ." I trailed off. "No, no, and no. Nothing in this one about pollutants."

Olivia and I had been holed up in the office for three hours. My parents were long since asleep, as was everyone else in the sanctuary. And for good reason—it was two in the morning. We'd snuck down after everyone went to bed.

It *had* to be a pollutant. Olivia and I agreed on that. We'd smelled that awful gassy smell twice— first on the day the dolphins arrived and then again when we were out on the boat. If it wasn't a leak, it was getting into the dolphin pen some other way. We just had to find out how.

"OK, look!" I held up a copy of *Updates on Environmental Toxins and Pollutants.*

"Ooh, good one." Olivia crawled over. "Ah, my leg's asleep." She propped herself next to me and looked over my shoulder.

"Hmm . . ." I stopped. "Oh my gosh. Wait. Just wait." I flipped through the pages, tearing a couple in my hurry until I came to the article. "'Louisiana Bayou Dumping Major Cause of Turtle Extinction.'"

Olivia looked at me like I was crazy. "Um, Elsa? We're not worried about turtles. Remember? They live in a tank here."

"Not the turtle part! Look! The dumping part!" I jabbed the page with my finger and read aloud: "Scientists were at first baffled by the presence of pollutants in the bayou waters as the plants nearby had been thoroughly inspected. But further investigation revealed that the polluters in question were hauling barrels to the bayou under cover of darkness and dumping the toxic chemicals into the fragile ecosystem." I inhaled. "Did you hear that? *Hauling barrels to the bayou and dumping the chemicals!*"

"Oh my gosh." Olivia was sitting straight up, her eyes wide, her hand covering her mouth. "Barrels."

I looked at Olivia. An image formed in my mind—the same image I knew Olivia was picturing. Blue barrels lined up in rows on a loading dock. Drips of liquid around them. A worker loading them into a—

"Olivia! A white van! Remember, that first morning we met Ms. Germaine? A *white van* had been blocking the driveway! The dolphin tech was complaining it was in his way, remember?"

Olivia suddenly stood up, the journal in her lap fluttering to the floor. "And there was a white van the morning of the ultrasound, remember? My sister was on the phone saying something to your mom about it! It seemed like nothing then."

"But it wasn't." My cheeks were burning, and my heart was beating fast. The pieces were coming together.

If we were right, CACM had been filling the barrels with some kind of pollutant and then hauling them to the cove at night to dump them. That's why we hadn't been able to find signs of a leak at the factory, I realized. There wasn't one.

I jumped up. "OK, but where are they dumping this stuff? They wouldn't do it right into the cove. It would be too risky to come into the sanctuary. They must be doing it close enough for the pollutant to get into the pens, but far enough away that they think they won't be detected. But where is that?"

Olivia was already pulling up a map of our section of coastline on her laptop. She clicked a couple of times, zooming in. "OK, here's us." Her finger traced the edge of the coast where Seaside

Sanctuary was located. "And here's the dolphin cove."

"What's over here?" I asked, motioning to a stetch of land not far away. Olivia had lived in Charleston way longer than me, so she knew the area better.

"These are cottages on the beach," she replied. Then she pointed to another section. "But there aren't any cottages on the other side. It's too close to the waterway. And the intracoastal waterway flows—"

"—right into the ocean," I finished.

"You mean, right into the cove," she said.

We both stared at each other. "I guess we know where to start looking."

Chapter 9

My alarm went off at 6 a.m. the next morning. In the early light, I pulled on a sweatshirt and leggings and crept from my room, past my parents' silent doorway, and out the front door.

Outside the ocean shushed back and forth in the gray dawn. The familiar smell of seaweed hung in the air. I jumped as something rustled near the feed bin, then exhaled as Olivia emerged.

"It's just you," I said, feeling relieved.

"Who were you expecting? Wonder Woman?" Olivia whispered back.

"Wonder Woman would be nice," I replied. "We could definitely use some superpowers right about now."

Silently we crept down the main path, toward the ocean. We turned right at the cove and made our way off of the sanctuary grounds and along the edge of the water. Luckily the Carolina coastline is pretty much the flattest place on Earth, so it wasn't hard to walk. We followed the beach past the summer cottages, all drawn tight and sleeping against the early sun.

Eventually the buildings fell away behind us, and the ground grew muddy and marshy beneath our feet. Marsh grasses stuck up everywhere along the banks. The ocean was only about twenty yards away, but it was clear this land belonged to the brackish intracoastal waterway. We'd have to walk carefully if we didn't want to suddenly sink knee-deep in fishy-smelling mud.

As we moved, the rising sun burned a red streak across the rippling water. Just then a heron rose out of the waters, and I caught my breath. He flapped his giant white wings and rose into the sky, legs dangling.

"What if they don't come?" I worried, as we picked our way along the bank. "Or what if we already missed them? Or what if we're in the wrong spot, and they're dumping PAHs somewhere else?"

"Then we'll sneak out every morning until we catch them," Olivia replied. She pulled a crumpled piece of paper from her pocket—the map she'd printed the day before—and checked it. "OK, I think this is far enough. I know we're just guessing at where they'll be dumping, but any farther and we'll be sitting in the waterway."

Suddenly I stopped. A faint trail led from the road far ahead, through the grasses, and into the waterway. It wasn't a cleared or marked trail—more like someone had forced their way through. Grasses had been trampled down and broken. And two faint wheel tracks, like those from a wagon, led straight to the mud at the water's edge.

"Do you see that?" I gasped, pointing.

Olivia stared. "I guess this is the right place. Let's just hope we're in time."

We found a place to sit and crouched together in the tall, damp grass. The air was already starting to grow hot, and humidity clung to us like a damp sweater. The grass and mud smelled like fish and decay and salt. It wasn't a bad smell—just strong.

We stared up at the path, waiting. As the minutes passed, my fast-beating heart slowed. My bottom was getting damp. I found myself thinking longingly of a shower and breakfast. Beside me, I could feel Olivia fidgeting in the itchy grass.

Suddenly I caught a glimpse of something white through the grasses and heard the faint sound of a motor. Seconds later, a white vehicle stopped on the blacktop.

I jerked upright. Olivia inhaled sharply and squeezed my arm, her fingernails digging in painfully. This was it.

In the silence, the dull clunk of a car door sounded. Then two figures appeared, fighting their way through the grasses, right on the trampled path we'd seen. They were pushing something before them on dollies. Barrels, I saw. Blue barrels with *CACM* stamped on the sides in black letters.

My breath was coming in short, rough gasps now. I crouched close to Olivia, our eyes glued to the figures. Without talking, the two men maneuvered the dollies through the mud, right up to the edge of the waterway. They were so close I could hear one of them grunt as he shifted the barrel off his dolly.

"Right in here?" he asked the other.

I looked at Olivia. My friend's eyes were huge. Neither of us dared move a finger.

"Yeah," the other answered. "Gimme that crowbar, will you?"

There was a little silence, then the sound of splashing as the liquid hit the water. Even from a distance, the stench of gas filled my nostrils.

Anger suddenly filled me. They were pouring that poison right into the water! It would flow straight down the waterway and into the cove. In ten minutes, maybe less, they'd be making the dolphins sick.

I wanted to jump up and scream at those men to stop, but Olivia's eyes pinned me down.

Stay quiet, she was saying. *Wait. We'll get them, don't worry.*

And so we waited, rigid and motionless, while the men balanced the now-empty barrels on the dollies again and trundled them back up the path. In minutes, they were gone. The whole thing had taken less than fifteen minutes.

I let out a huge breath I didn't know I'd been holding and looked at Olivia. "We did it!" my friend scream-whispered.

"We don't have to whisper anymore." I stood up. "We did it!" I called toward the ocean, joy filling me. "Star! Ruby! We did it!"

But then I remembered the dolphins, who would soon be bathing in a pool of poison. There was no time to celebrate.

"Olivia, quick! We have to tell your sister and my parents before the dolphins get any sicker!"

We ran as fast as we could back through the grasses, toward the beach, and then on to the sanctuary's entrance.

"Did you see the logo on the barrels? Those men must work at CACM," I said as we scurried along. "Ms. Germaine is the plant manager. She has to know about the dumping."

"Do you think she told them to do it?" Olivia asked.

"I don't know. Remember when she first came out here? She seemed really surprised—and upset—to see the dolphins in the wild pen. Maybe she didn't order the dumping, but she probably knew about it. Otherwise why would she care enough to be upset?"

"That makes sense. But right now, all I want is to help Star and Ruby," Olivia said as we panted up the hill to the houses. "We can deal with her later."

"Agreed," I said as we reached the office. Abby's apartment was above it, and my house was just beyond. We banged on the door. "Abby! Mom! Dad!" I yelled. "Help!"

After a moment, we heard feet thudding on the stairs, and Abby wrenched the door open. I could see Mom hurrying toward us from the house, tying the belt of her old bathrobe as she moved.

"Elsa?" Abby peered out, her hair sticking up. "Olivia? What are you doing out so early?"

"Abby," I said. "We have something to tell you."

❧

"Hurry!" Mom shouted. "Someone get up to the top of the drive and direct the techs down here!"

It was only a few hours later, but Seaside Sanctuary had become more like Seaside Rescue.

Staff and volunteers were scrambling everywhere, preparing to move the remaining dolphins from the wild pen to our largest saltwater pool.

Everyone was doing their part. Abby was testing the water content of the freshly filled pool, Dad was gassing up the motorboats, and Olivia and I had been dragging out the body mats we'd need to move the dolphins onto the floating stretchers. We dropped the mats and scrambled up the drive, just as the big Marine transport van pulled in.

"This way!" I called to the driver, motioning down the drive. We jogged after the van, arriving just as the van pulled up to the cove.

The techs jumped out and flung open the doors, dragging out the floating stretchers. "Everything ready in the new location?" one of them asked Mom.

"Ready," Mom said, nodding. "Let's get the animals out of there."

I knew Mom was as eager as I was to get Ruby and Star away from that poisoned water. Without hesitation, she jumped into one of the motorboats with Dad and the techs. Olivia and I watched from the edge as they gently put-putted out to the dolphins, who were floating limply in the water.

As we watched, the techs unfurled the floating mats and eased them under the dolphins' bodies. Then, using the mats as support, they maneuvered the dolphins onto floating stretchers alongside the boats. Once the animals were secure, Mom and Dad carefully steered the boats back to the dock, the dolphins floating on stretchers right beside them.

"OK, let's get them up to safety," Dad said as they climbed from the boats.

The techs disconnected the stretchers and carefully lifted the dolphins from the water. Working quickly, they stretchered them from the cove up to the newly filled pool.

Olivia and I ran alongside, careful to stay out of the way. It broke my heart to see the animals like this. Their eyes were half-closed, and I could hear them wheezing. They looked so sick.

"Hang on, guys," I whispered. "Just hang on. You're almost there."

At the saltwater pool—full of clear, good-smelling water—the techs reversed the procedure. They climbed into the pool and stood waist-deep while they eased the stretchers out from under the dolphins. Star and Ruby were able to support their own weight, but just barely.

"You're going to get better—I promise," I whispered to the dolphins, leaning over the edge of the pool.

Olivia heard me and reached out for my hand, giving it a reassuring squeeze. "That's a promise we're going to be able to keep."

Chapter 10

The following afternoon, Olivia and I sat with
Abby, my parents, and Ms. Germaine in front of
the saltwater pool. Star and Ruby swam in gentle
circles in the sparkling water, blowing occasionally
and chirping gently. Already their sores looked
better. Abby said they were less congested too.

Ms. Germaine looked less content. She was
sitting rigidly in her folding chair, hands knotted

together in her lap. She didn't make eye contact with any of us.

"Ms. Germaine," Mom said tightly. "I have done you a favor by calling you here so that you can explain yourself *before* I call the police. That's only because of your work at Wildlife Resources. But I will be calling them, regardless of what you say. However, if you would like to offer some explanation for the poisonings—not to mention the death of our dolphin—my husband and I will allow you that."

I don't think I'd ever seen Mom so angry. She looked like she was ready to spring up out of her chair and push Ms. Germaine right into the dolphin pool.

I didn't think anyone would stop her.

Ms. Germaine kept her gaze on the concrete. "Thank you for that," she said in a low voice. "I-I'm terribly sorry."

The words meant nothing to me. Not after all that had happened to our animals. I could tell Mom felt the same.

"What I don't understand," Mom continued, "is why you would knowingly pollute our waters and hurt our animals? Why? And why couldn't we detect the chemical when we tested the water for pollutants?"

"I think I can answer part of that, Mae," Abby broke in, possibly to keep Mom from actually throwing Ms. Germaine into the water. "I've been on the phone with pollutant experts since last night. This morning we ran a few tests. Elsa and Olivia were right: CACM was dumping a chemical called PAH. It's dangerous, but it also evaporates out of the water quickly. The dolphins were affected when it was dumped, especially since it was inhaled from the surface of the water. That explains their respiratory symptoms."

"But that doesn't explain why it didn't show up on the previous tests," Dad said.

"By the time we tested, it had dispersed," Abby continued. "Elsa and Olivia were often the first ones down in the morning, so they were smelling it just after it was dumped. And since the chemical was dumped instead of leaked steadily, the waters were only polluted occasionally."

Ms. Germaine looked down at her hands. "I cannot tell you how deeply I regret my part in this. You're right. I knew about the dumping and did nothing to stop it. I knew at the factory you were looking for a leak, when the whole time the answer was right there at the loading dock."

Anger swept through me, almost taking my breath away. "How could you do this to us? To the animals? They suffered! Sunshine died!" Angry tears fell from my eyes. Out of the corner of my eye I could see Olivia staring at Ms. Germaine, her own eyes watery.

Ms. Germaine swiped tears from her cheeks. "My only reason—which is not an excuse—is that Mr. Stanton, the factory owner, is a difficult man. He threatened to fire me if I breathed a word about the dumping or tried to stop it in any way. Disposing of PAH is expensive. Stanton saw the dumping as a cheap and easy solution. He told me that the ocean was big and the small amount we dumped wouldn't hurt anyone. But when I saw the dolphins in their wild pen, I knew. I knew the chemical would leak in."

"So why didn't you do anything?" Mom asked coldly.

"I tried. I told Stanton I would go to the Agriculture and Fisheries Department and the press. But then . . ." Ms. Germaine looked down. "He threatened me. He said he'd fire me, and I'd never get another job in Charleston. I have a son, and I'm all on my own. I need this job. So I kept quiet. I know it was wrong. This secret has eaten me alive since the moment I found out about the dumping. I'm not asking you to forgive me or even to understand. I just want you to know how very, *very* sorry I am for my part in this."

For a long time, no one said anything. Then Dad broke the silence.

"The good news is that the dolphins will recover," he said. "And they should suffer no long-term effects. But Sunshine is gone forever—and Seaside Sanctuary's reputation as a safe place for marine life has been badly damaged by the negative publicity."

"Oh, I know!" Ms. Germaine said. "Please, please let me do whatever I can to fix that." She looked right at Olivia and me. "I'll confess to the police and to the Agricultural and Fisheries

Department about the part that I played. I'll tell them everything. I'll make sure they know Seaside Sanctuary is blameless. That's the least I can do."

Epilogue

Olivia and I saw Ms. Germaine one last time, about a week after the dolphin rescue. She stopped by the sanctuary as Olivia and I were scrubbing the sides of the saltwater pool. The dolphins were swimming around us—blowing playfully out of their blowholes, diving to the bottom of the pool, then leaping out of the water. Their sores had healed as fast as Dad said they would, and their breathing was back to normal.

It was almost like things *were* back to normal. But the loss of Sunshine still weighed on me when I thought of her.

By the time Olivia and I climbed out of the pool and pulled shorts over our swimsuits, Ms. Germaine and Mom were deep in conversation. Ms. Germaine was dressed as I'd never seen her, in jeans and a T-shirt, with her hair in a ponytail. She almost looked like a different person.

Mom looked over at me as we approached. "Ms. Germaine came to say goodbye," she said. "She's taken a job in South America."

"I told the police everything. They've decided not to press charges against me," Ms. Germaine said. "I'm very grateful. But I'll still have trouble finding a job in the area when my connection to CACM comes out. My son and I are going to stay with my sister in Brazil for a while."

"What about Mr. Stanton?" I asked.

Ms. Germaine looked serious. "He was arrested. He's out on bail, but he'll stand trial for illegal dumping and endangering wildlife. The factory will be fined and closed for inspection. I don't know if it will survive, or if he'll have to close it."

"Good!" Olivia said fiercely. I felt the same way, although I didn't say anything.

Ms. Germaine held her hand out to Mom, who hesitated a moment before finally shaking it. Then she held her hand out to me. I wanted to refuse it. I was still so angry about what she'd done. But she looked at me, straight and steady. I shook her hand.

"I've learned my lesson," Ms. Germaine said softly to us. "It's wrong to stand by when innocent animals are being harmed. I'm sorry I wasn't braver. I wish I had been."

"Me too," I told her. "But at least you're doing something now. I'm glad everything is out in the open now."

"That's right," Olivia agree. "No more secrets."

"And no more adventures," I said as we watched Ms. Germaine walk back up the path to her car. "At least—for a little while."

About the Author

Emma Carlson Berne is the author of many books for children and young adults. She loves writing about history, plants and animals, outdoor adventures, and sports. Emma lives in Cincinnati, Ohio, with her husband and three little boys. When she's not writing, Emma likes to ride horses, hike, and read books to her sons.

About the Illustrator

Erwin Madrid grew up in San Jose, California, and earned his BFA in Illustration from the Academy of Art College in San Francisco. During his final semester, Erwin was hired by PDI/DreamWorks Animation, where he contributed production art for *Shrek 2*. He later became a visual development artist for the Shrek franchise, the *Madagascar* sequel, and *Megamind*. He has designed cover art for children's books from Harper Collins, Random House, and Simon and Schuster. He currently lives in the Bay Area.

Glossary

anthropomorphize (an-thruh-puh-MAWR-fahyz)—to attribute human form or personality to non-human objects or things such as animals or plants

captivity (kap-TIV-i-tee)—held or confined so as to prevent escape

dispersed (dis-pursd)—widely spread or scattered

ecosystem (EK-oh-sis-tuhm)—a system made up of an ecological community of living things interacting with their environment, especially under natural conditions

lethargic (luh-THAHR-jik)—abnormal drowsiness

pollutant (puh-LOOT-nt)—something that pollutes or contaminates its surroundings

sanctuary (SANGK-choo-er-ee)—a place that provides shelter or protection

Talk About It

1. Early in the book, Elsa notes that people often think dolphins are smiling because of the way their faces look. Is there any danger in believing an animal is smiling or behaving in another human-like way? Why should people be cautious of this?

2. Why do you think Elsa and Olivia don't suspect Ms. Germaine of being involved with the dumping at first? Did the fact that her company—Charleston Area Chemical Manufacturing—gave money to Seaside Sanctuary affect Elsa and Olivia's thinking?

3. Dolphins are often affected by pollutants in our oceans. Think of an animal population that lives near you. How would pollution, either in the air, on land, or in the water, affect this population? What's one thing you could do to help?

Write About It

1. Pretend that you're in Elsa's shoes. Write a letter to the authorities, describing how Mr. Stanton's actions and illegal dumping impacted Seaside Sanctuary.

2. Imagine that you get to help out at Seaside Sanctuary in the same way Elsa and Olivia do. Which animal would you be most excited to interact with? Write a few paragraphs about the animal you chose. Make sure to include your reasons for choosing that animal.

3. Do you think offshore sea pens, like the one described in this book, are a good option for dolphins and whales that once lived in captivity? Do some research on the pros and cons and write a paragraph explaining your conclusion and opinion.

More About Dolphins

Dolphins aren't just beautiful—they're also some of the most intelligent animals on the planet. (Did you know they have the ability to learn and pass their knowledge on to other dolphins?) Here are ten more facts that might surprise you:

1. There are more than forty dolphin species in the world (although some are extinct). Most are in the ocean, but seven species live in rivers.

2. Dolphins are part of the family of whales that includes orcas—also known as killer whales. In fact, the biggest dolphin in the world is the killer whale!

3. In the wild, dolphins can live at least forty years. (Orcas can live at least seventy years!) However, dolphins kept in captivity don't live nearly as long.

4. Dolphins are highly social animals—they live and travel in groups called pods. Pods can have anywhere from two to thirty members, although superpods of up to a thousand dolphins can form in areas rich with food.

5. A dolphin calf will stay with its mother for up to eight years.

6. Dolphins are carnivores—they survive on a diet of fish, squid, shrimp, jellyfish, and octopus.

7. All dolphins have teeth, but they don't chew their food like humans do. Instead, they grab, bite, and swallow.

8. Dolphins use a complex system of sounds—including clicks, squeaks, and whistles—to communicate.

9. Dolphins use echolocation to hunt. They send out sounds and listen to the echo, which tells them exactly what's around them and where their prey is.

10. The United States Navy has trained and used bottlenose dolphins since 1960, when they first studied Notty, a female Pacific white-sided dolphin. Dolphins are still used for tasks including locating underwater mines and enemy swimmers.

Seaside SANCTUARY

When 12-year-old Elsa Roth's parents uproot their family and move them from Chicago, Illinois, to a seaside marine biology facility in Charleston, South Carolina, she expects to be lonely and bored. Little does she know that Seaside Sanctuary might just be the most interesting place she could have imagined. Whether she's exploring her new home, getting to know an amazing animal, or basking in the sun, Elsa realizes there's fun to be had—and mysteries to be solved—at Seaside Sanctuary.

Read all of Elsa's seaside adventures!

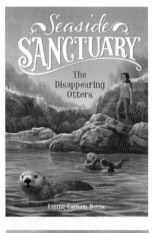

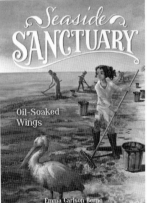

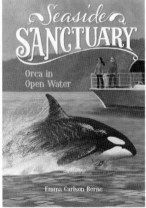

3/25/19

Use FactHound to find Internet sites related to this book.

Visit www.facthound.com
Just type in **9781496578594** and go.